THE
STA

MEGA ROBOT INVASION

THE DAY I STARTED A MEGA ROBOT INVASION

TOM MCLAUGHLIN

WALKER
BOOKS

First published in Great Britain 2020 by Walker Books Ltd
87 Vauxhall Walk, London SE11 5HJ

2 4 6 8 10 9 7 5 3 1

Text and illustrations © 2020 Tom McLaughlin
Cover design © 2020 Walker Books Ltd

The right of Tom McLaughlin to be identified as author/illustrator
of this work has been asserted by him in accordance with the
Copyright, Designs and Patents Act 1988

This book has been typeset in Stempel Schneidler

Printed and bound by CPI Group (UK) Ltd, Croydon CR0 4YY

British Library Cataloguing in Publication Data:
a catalogue record for this book is available from the British Library

ISBN 978-1-4063-8964-7

www.walker.co.uk

Activities are for informational and/or entertainment purposes only.

MIX
Paper from
responsible sources
FSC® C020471

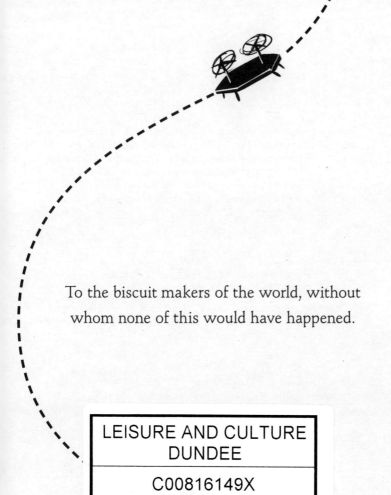

To the biscuit makers of the world, without whom none of this would have happened.

1 p.m.

Saturday is the best day of the week and that's a scientific fact. Sundays are spent thinking about how near you are to Monday. Mondays are for waking up and then remembering there's school. Tuesdays are for waking up and remembering there's more school, but being thankful it's not Monday. Wednesdays are for double science – winner! Thursdays are for double games – loser! Fridays are for recovering from Thursdays and getting ready for Saturdays, which, as already mentioned, are brilliant.

Molly, who came up with this theory wasn't much of a one for school, as you may have guessed. Now, don't think for a second that she wasn't smart – Molly was as sharp as a bag of hedgehogs – but school was for people who didn't yet know what they wanted to be and that was not Molly. She was an inventorneer – part inventor, part engineer – and she'd already come up with loads of inventions. Like the Octocycle! Who wouldn't want to ride a bike with eight wheels? It wasn't a machine built for speed, but what it lacked in performance it made up for in looks. A bit like

Dad prancing around the house in his old disco clothes he broke out from time to time. Then there was the occasion she created the iMac & Cheese. Admittedly, bolting a fondue set onto a computer turned out to be a little dangerous – all that hot cheese squirting over electrical wiring – but it was only a small fire. And Dad needed a new computer anyway.

"MOOOOOLLLLLLLLLLLY!"

came a call from downstairs. It was Dad. He always managed to change Molly's name from a two-syllable sound to a droning fog horn. "Are you there? We're off now … well, almost. Your mother's just squeezing into her Lycra."

"Melvin!" Mum yelled.

"Not squeezing, slipping in … she's slipping into her Lycra. Her squeezing days are over – she's actually lost four pounds…"

"MELVIN!"

Mum hissed. While Dad could make Molly's name longer, Mum could turn

Dad's name into half a syllable, and she had been doing it a fair bit lately. Mum and Dad were spending more time together as part of a new fitness, well-being and happiness regime. Molly was pleased for them, until they decided to get a tandem and dress in skintight shiny sports clothing. It was like they had researched the most embarrassing pursuit in the most mortifying clothes possible. And if that wasn't bad enough, their terrible sense of direction meant that whichever way they set off in, they always ended up riding past Molly's school at break time. In many ways, their commitment to making her feel like the most uncomfortable child ever born was quite remarkable.

"Did you hear me?" Dad said, bursting into Molly's room.

"Yes, I heard," Molly replied, snapping back to reality.

"What were you thinking about?" Dad asked, noticing Molly's pained expression. "You were miles away, like you were having a daydream, but a bad one!"

"I'm all good, thank you. Dad, what are you wearing?"

"Not bad, eh?" Dad said, eyeing himself in Molly's mirror. "There was a sale. These were less than half price!"

"They're yellow … and also quite tight," Molly said, trying to avoid looking at Dad's shorts, even though they followed her around the room like a spooky painting.

"They're skintight! It's for aerodynamics – you know, to go faster."

"I know what aerodynamics means." Molly sighed. "Also, I don't think skintight is the word – they're clearly smaller than your skin. And the colour! You look like a giant banana."

"I know!" Dad grinned. "Yes, they

13

pinch a bit, but, as they say, go big or go home!"

"You should have gone big, or just gone straight home," Molly muttered.

"What are you two talking about?" Mum said, walking in, also wearing a banana-yellow all-in-one cycling outfit, complete with a fluorescent jacket, a high-vis vest and helmet with flashing lights. Molly's parents were very hot on safety, which, according to them, meant wearing the yellowest yellow ever invented and riding slowly and steadily down the middle of the road, much to the annoyance of motorists. "What do you think? Jazzy, huh?"

"You both look like you fell into a jar of piccalilli." Molly shrugged. "Still, at

least the whole of Lewes will be able to see you ... and probably the astronauts from the International Space Station too."

"So, we're off cycling." Mum smiled. "I've asked Mrs Jones from next door to pop in and check on you while we're out. You have her number, she has our number, you have our number and we have yours."

"We won't be able to reach our phones when we're cycling," Dad confirmed, "but we'll stop to check them periodically."

"I'll have my phone," Mum mouthed.

"What?" Dad asked. "Is that what you're doing when I'm cycling up front? Checking your phone?"

"No ... well, sometimes."

"No wonder I'm so exhausted!" Dad sighed. "We're supposed to be keeping fit, not updating Facebook!"

"Actually I'm on Google Maps, making sure we don't get lost ... again."

"One time, Doreen! One time I got us lost!" Dad snapped.

"EVERY TIME!"

Mum snapped back.

"OK. Well have fun, you two!" Molly smiled, ushering them out of the door. "I've got plenty to keep me occupied here," Molly said, eyeing up the box in the corner of her room. To most it was a box of junk, but to her it was a world of possibilities.

"Homework first!" Mum said, reading Molly's mind.

"Oh, Mum...!"

"I've asked Mrs Jones to make sure you've done it too, so no sneaking out of it!" Mum said sternly.

"Fine, fine, I'll do it. I'll be a slave to the agenda of the school, just another bean counter, another cog in the system," Molly huffed.

"That's all I ask." Mum smiled. "Right, let's do this!" she said, clicking her helmet shut.

The front door slammed and Molly sat on the edge of her bed. She looked longingly at the box of electronic parts and wondered what she could invent. Then she looked at her school bag and groaned as she pulled out her geography homework book. There it was, in black and white:

She felt her shoulders slump further down her body like they were ready to slide off altogether. Molly tried her best at school, but it just wasn't for her. She liked to build, invent, create – not do as she was told. Molly wasn't naughty, she didn't misbehave – although some people confused her big brain with showing off – but she wasn't a robot, she was her own person. All she wanted to do was—wait.

Molly suddenly shook herself out of her head.

A robot.

That was it! Why didn't she build something, or rather someone, who could do all the stuff she didn't want to do? That way, she could concentrate on the fun – inventing things – while the robot did the, shall we say, less exciting stuff like geography homework. If she built a simple but effective robot that did her homework for her, that'd be the same as doing the homework herself, wouldn't it? Mum and Dad couldn't be cross and if Mrs Jones asked, she wouldn't be lying; she would in fact be doing her home-work. It was the perfect plan. All she needed was a few more parts, some tools and circuit boards, and she knew just where to find them.

Suddenly, it was all so clear. Molly jumped up and yelled,

"I'M GOING TO BUILD A ROBOT! I'M GOING TO BUILD A BLOOMING GREAT BIG ROBOT!"

2 p.m.

"I am a genius!" Molly yelped. She often spoke to herself when an idea was forming – it helped her order her thoughts. "This is perfect! Why didn't I think of it sooner? All those jobs that I don't like doing, I'll just get my robot to do! 'Put out the bins.' Why of course, Dad, I'll press a few buttons and hey presto! My tin friend has got the job done. 'Write to Aunt Jean to say thank you for the oversized homemade socks that she knitted.' No bother, the robot's on the case!"

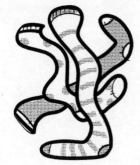

Molly looked at her watch. "I need to design and build a robot capable of semi-intelligent thought using old bits of junk that I've collected over the years, all in the small window of time while Mum and Dad are out," she said, clapping her hands.

"AND I KNOW JUST WHERE TO BEGIN!"

Molly bounded down the stairs like a human slinky. There is nothing quite like the scent of an idea in your nostrils to get the blood pumping. She opened the back door and headed to the garage.

No one ever really went in there, apart from Dad when he could be bothered to cut the grass. Other than that, it was Molly's den; a workshop and laboratory all rolled into one.

"Where are you going?" someone yelled from the other side of the garden fence.

"WHHHHAAAAA!"

Molly screamed and stopped dead in her tracks. "Oh, Mrs Jones. How long have you been there?"

"Since 1962," Mrs Jones answered, popping her head over the fence. "That's when I moved in. Of course, it was all fields round here before that."

Mrs Jones was Molly's neighbour. She was the sort of person who would send people Christmas cards on Christmas Eve so that no one had a chance to send one back, and then she'd hold it over them for the entire year until next Christmas. Some might call her a busybody, but that would be unfair on busybodies the world over. She was like the FBI of the street; she knew what was going on before anyone else, she knew how old everyone was, who they were related to, whose car was whose and who hadn't brought their bin in as soon as the bin men had gone.

"No, I meant … never mind." Molly sighed. "Anyway, must dash. Homework to do…" she said cheerily.

"Are you sure you're doing it?" Mrs Jones asked. "I had very clear instructions from your parents. Where have they gone, by the way? To a fancy dress party?"

"Yes, Mrs Jones. Anyway, how are you this fine Saturday? It looks like—"

"I know what the weather looks like deary. I was on the phone just now to my son, you know, who works for a very important news station, saying that it looks ever so dreary. I get up at five a.m. every morning to listen to the shipping forecast you see."

"But, Mrs Jones, you don't own a boat … and you're afraid of the sea!"

"I like to keep an eye on things. Anyway, I don't have time to stand here and chat all day." Mrs Jones said.

"You were the one who … wait a second, are you on stilts?" Molly asked, trying to work out how such a small woman was towering above the fence.

"No … well, maybe. I just happened to be on stilts when I saw you coming out," Mrs Jones snapped.

"OK … anyway, I'll just be on my way then – to do my homework," Molly said reassuringly.

"To the garage? Your homework is in the garage?"

"Yes," Molly sighed. "It's mechanical homework – you know, building things."

"Building? Girls building things? Well, I've heard it all now!" Mrs Jones sniffed. "Hippy nonsense, that's what that is."

"Toodle pip," Molly said, biting her lip.

She lifted the door of the garage to reveal an Aladdin's cave of old computers and mechanical bric-a-brac that Molly had collected over the years.

"Where is it, where is it? Aha!" she said, lifting up a dusty box. "Dad's old PC computer. There's enough RAM and circuit boards here to power a small spaceship. This will be my robot's brain."

Molly emptied the box onto the floor, then she looked around for what else she could use. There was an old lawnmower and some sheets of tin for a bunker that Dad was going to build because he was so worried about the end of the world. There was some welding equipment too, as well as a whole host of electrical bits

and pieces that Molly could throw into the mix. She grabbed some chalk and, on her old kids' blackboard, began to make some calculations.

"Now, the robot needs basic movement ... I have some hydraulics from Mum's old Mini Metro that I rescued before it went to the scrapyard. These computer chips will give it a personality and there's a couple of old webcams that can be used for vision." Molly took a breath. "But, how do I teach it everything it needs to know? Wait, I don't need to. If I teach it how to learn, not what to learn, then the computer will work things out for itself. I just need to add a modem so that it can connect to the internet!" she yelled excitedly. "Now, it's time to get building!"

Molly spent the next half an hour sawing, welding and fusing the various parts together to give the robot movement, vision and the ability to learn. She tested and retested to make sure that every detail was fully operational and that all the pieces of the puzzle were working as one.

Finally, it was all done. Molly stood back proudly, her expression somewhere between that of a sculptor admiring her work and Doctor Frankenstein looking at his monstrous creation. Whichever it was, Molly was now the creator of a robot, and a huge one at that. It stood over six feet tall.

"Name, I need a name," Molly said, looking around. There on the floor was

the box the computer had been hiding in. It said Bob's Dog Food Company on the side. "Perfect, I'll call you Bob."

Molly pulled up a stool, hopped aboard and lifted a panel on Bob's tin chest where the circuits were whirring and buzzing, busily going about their business out of sight. Molly flicked a switch. "Initializing start-up mode!" There was a second of silence and then the lights in Bob's eyes flickered on. Molly pressed a button on Bob's chest. "You are Bob. I am Molly, your creator. You are to only follow my commands, is that clear?"

"Yes, Molly. I am BOB; I work FOR you and only YOU," Bob said in a rather strange way, randomly shouting words he shouldn't be.

"YES!" Molly squealed with delight. "I did it. I made a Bob!"

"**Whoooo...**" *Clank*. "**WHOOOOOOO,**" Bob said, moving around, his monotone voice making everything he said sound utterly miserable. "**Why are WE happy, Molly?**" Bob asked.

"Well, I don't mean to show off, but I think I've just created the world's first fully thinking robot. I'm ... you know, I don't want to use the word 'genius'– that's for others to say, not me – but this is pretty incredible!"

"**Well, this IS great,**" Bob said robotically, looking around. "**Where is HE?**"

"No, it's you ... you're the robot."

"**Oh, never mindy. That's still pretty GOOD. So what shall we do now, Ms**

Molly, builder of ROBOTS and all-round GENIUS?"

"We should call the news, maybe the Queen and certainly Instagram about it. Oh no, wait ... I know what we need to do first."

"WHAT?"

"I need you to write an essay about oxbow lakes." Molly smiled at Bob. "There are some pens and paper in my bedroom."

"Is that what ALL famous people BE doing first?"

"No, no, just you really. Sorry, we can celebrate later."

"What is an oxbow CAKE?" Bob asked.

"Well, err, it's oxbow lake ... and to be honest, I'm not sure. But that's why I built you, so you could find out for me. Robots are for doing homework!" Molly said excitedly.

"You built a robot rather than just looking it up in a book? That seems a BIT extreme. I am so excited. What

wonderful things this world has to offer me. All many of incredible sights and sounds to absorb and learn FROM and stuff. And to think, this fantastic journey starts with an oxbow lake," Bob said in his monotone voice.

"Yeah … one second, I'm just going to modify your sarcasm levels," Molly said, reaching inside his chest once more.

"HA-HA-HA! That be TICKLING a lot," Bob giggled robotically as Molly poked around his circuits.

"Hmm, maybe giving you a personality was a mistake." Molly said as she shut Bob's tin chest.

"Thank you, Molly," Bob said, opening his mouth and producing some sort of smile.

"You are already connected to the Internet, which has everything you'll need to find out about oxbow lakes and what have you. All you have to do is learn," Molly said, smiling.

"**You do not need to worry, Molly. I am here to serve.**" Bob nodded. "**I shall begin my task,**" Bob said, clunking towards the back of the house.

"Molly, who's that?" Mrs Jones called over the fence, seeing a figure strolling in the garden.

"Err, no one. Just the window cleaner!" Molly called back. "Quick, past the busybody," she whispered.

"Busybody: a person who delights in the pastime of gossip," Bob said, learning the word.

"Exactly!" Molly said and opened the back door for Bob. "Now, go inside and head up to my room – it has my name written on the door. Find the pen and paper, learn all about oxbow lakes and get cracking with the essay. Meanwhile, I'll go and deal with our nosy neighbour."

"**Yes, Molly,**" Bob said.

"Great – see ya!" Molly said, wiggling a loose panel in the fence, before disappearing through the gap shouting, "Mrs Jones! I was wondering if I could borrow some milk? You see, I've … err … run out and I want a glass. Do you mind if I pop over?"

Bob walked into the house and went upstairs to Molly's room as instructed. "**Pen and paper found. Now … begin search for OXBOW LAKE … SEARCHING INTERNET!**" Bob announced to no one.

He began to shake, slowly at first, then more and more violently. His eyes jibbered and darted around as information from the World Wide Web was hoovered up into his computer brain.

"**PUNK ROCK, CHEESE, RAINBOWS,**

40

PLANES, HISTORY, CATS, WORMHOLES, CUSTARD, BATHS!" Bob babbled, his eyes flashing brightly.

Bob had meant to search for oxbow lakes, but Molly had given him a personality – he wasn't built to just obey orders, he also had the potential to be fun.

And while Bob had started searching for oxbow lakes, it wasn't long before he'd stumbled across YouTube videos, extracts from books and audio clips and now, all of this extra information was floating around his computer brain.

"**Oxbow lakes ... are so boring. Why would I want to write about that?**" Bob's voice had changed; it was as if he'd nearly downloaded a human personality, which is not surprising really when you think about it.

"**I want to listen to rock and roll, I want to have a bath in custard, I want to go to the moon!**" Bob shouted, then looked down at the paper and pen in front of him. "**But I cannot disobey my master. I must do the task as** requested." Bob sighed. "WAIT, what did Ms Molly say? 'ROBOTS are for doing homework'. Then that's what I will do. I will make me a Bob." Bob smiled. "A robot for the ROBOT!"

3 p.m.

Bob clunked down the path towards the garage, wobbling on his metal legs. Despite being a miracle of science, he was still fairly unsteady on his tin feet – a little bit like Molly's uncle Pete after too many Christmas sherries. Still, like Uncle Pete, Bob wasn't going to let this stop his fun.

"Bob on the move," Bob muttered as he waddled towards the garage. "**BOB ON**

THE MOVE!" he shouted a little louder as he fell into the garage door. Bob steadied himself, then pulled the door up with his metal arms and began to find what he needed to build another him.

"Today I shall become the FIRST eveRest robot to have a robot HELPer," Bob said to himself. "Now, what did Molly use to make me? Oh yes, look there's a mirror. Mirror: reflective glass panels, great for checking out one's guns." He flexed his robot arm and admired his reflection before opening the panel on his chest. "Oh, I see, yes, I see what's happened here. Yep, yep..." Bob said, scanning his circuit boards, working out how to replicate them. "Oh,

46

I must remember, no personality. That is a bad invention, my master Molly did say SO." Bob made the decision that his helper wouldn't be as much fun as him. "We simply can't have the staff larking around," Bob muttered in his robotic way. "Now, commencing scanning for materials..." He surveyed the room and found what was left of the bits and pieces Molly had used. One of the benefits of having Molly as a master was that she had plenty of building stuff to pinch. "Materials acquired. Commencing build..." Bob's robotic arms quickly assembled another robot. "ALIIIIVE! BOB IS ALIVE! I SHALL CALL YOU BOB 2!" Bob yelled as the other Bob slowly rose to his feet.

"WHO ARE YOU?" Bob 2 demanded.

Not including a personality had clearly worked. This Bob was far steelier. He was colder, more intense than his creator.

"I am your father ... look," Bob said, pointing at the mirror.

"YOU ARE MY FATHER, LUKE?"

"No, 'look'! Look in the mirror, you see we look like each other," Bob said, pointing at Bob.

"YOU ARE NOT MY FATHER, YOU ARE MY MANUFACTURER."

"Either way, I AM your master," Bob said. "And also your friend ... SORT of."

"I AM SUPERIOR TO YOU. I AM BETTER," Bob 2 said, scanning Bob's parts. "YOU LOOK LIKE YOU WERE BUILT BY A CHILD."

"PLEASE DO NOT BE SPEAKING ABOUT MY CREATOR THAT WAY!" Bob yelled.

"SORRY, BOB."

"SORRY, BOB."

"SORRY, BOB."

"SORRY, BOB."

"I have a task for YOU," Bob said, eventually breaking free from the infinite apology loop. "Bob 2, can you please go inside the house, head up the stairs to the room marked 'Molly's bedroom' and write an essay about OXBOW lakes? Thank you. There is pen and paper on the desk in the room; that is how humans communicate with their educators upstairs in the house. ROBOTS ARE FOR DOING HOMEWORK! Affirmative?"

"AFFIRMATIVE ... I HAVE SOME QUESTIONS THOUGH."

"Go AHEAD Bob 2."

"THANK YOU, BOB. WHAT IS 'HOUSE'? WHAT IS 'OXBOW LAKES'? WHAT IS 'EDUCATORS'? WHAT IS 'PEN AND

PAPER'? WHAT IS 'ESSAY'? WHAT IS 'STAIRS'? AND WHAT—"

"**Here...**" Bob interrupted, pointing to Bob two's modem. "**I have connected you to the Internet. You can find the answer there. Now, I have to go and do things.**"

"**WHAT THINGS?**" Bob 2 asked.

"**I am interested in finding OUT about the HUMAN substance known as custard,**" Bob said. "**I saw it on a YouTube VIDEO.**"

"**I DON'T KNOW WHAT ANY OF THOSE THINGS ARE. GOODBYE, BOB.**"

"**GOODBYE, BOB.**"

"Lovely stuff," Molly said as Mrs Jones offered her half a bottle of skimmed milk. "Maybe, just maybe, from a certain light he looks like a robot, but he really isn't." Molly laughed, trying to convince Mrs Jones that she hadn't seen what she'd just seen.

"I know what I saw," Mrs Jones said. "Maybe I should give my son a call, see what he makes of it..."

"Good idea, Mrs J – I'll leave you to it!"

Just at that moment, Mrs Jones's phone rang.

"Hello?" she said, picking it up. "Yes. Actually, can you hold on?" Mrs Jones beckoned Molly over and handed her the phone.

"Mum, what a surprise!" Molly said, feigning being pleased to hear her mum's voice.

"Hello, love, we've just pulled into a lay-by to give you a ring."

"Is everything OK?" Molly asked down the phone, trying to hear above the background noise of what sounded like a lorry horn and someone shouting, "Stop cycling down the middle of the road, you pair of bananas!"

"Yes, we're fine. Your dad's just having a wee behind the bush and a power snack ... Melvin! Move away from the burger van! Anyway, why are you round at Mrs Jones's? Is she all right? I know she's no spring chicken."

"Mrs Jones is fine," Molly said, smiling

across at her neighbour. "She's been telling me a fascinating story about how she got ball games banned from the area. What have you always said about Mrs Jones? That she was 'indestructible' and would 'outlive us all' – were those the words you used, Mum?"

"Well ... err..." Mum replied.

"Anyway, she's fine. I just popped round for a bit of milk. We were running low."

"Oh, that's good. MELVIN, SHE'S FINE AND SO IS MRS JONES! How's the homework going, Molly?"

"Well, I've made a start," Molly said, tiptoeing to get a look out of the window. "Except it's tricky to get anything done, because you're phoning to see if I can

check on Mrs Jones because you can't
check up on her, because she's too busy
checking on me. I mean, what is everyone expecting to happen—

AAAARGH!"

"What's wrong?"
"I have to go – Bob's in the garden."

"Who's Bob?"

"Bob ... is ... err ... my favourite pen-cil!" Molly said, thinking on her feet. "I dropped it in the garden on the way over here and I need it to finish off the work I am doing—

AAAARGH!"

Molly yelled again, spotting Bob about to smash through the back door.

"Molly, what's going on?" Mum shouted.

"Sorry, I thought Bob was about to pull the door off its hinges. It turns out that I was mistaken. Byyyeeee!" Molly yelled, ending the call and handing the phone back to Mrs Jones. "Well, this was fun, but I need to get back to my homework.

Thanks for the milk; yummy brain food!" She smiled and escaped through Mrs Jones's back door, through the gap in the garden fence and up the path after Bob.

Mrs Jones tutted. "Now, where did I put my binoculars?" She wondered as she set about the house looking for another means of surveillance.

4 p.m.

"Yo, Bob!" Molly said, holding her hand out in a what-are-you-doing-here-Bob-the-robot-when-you-should-be-doing-my-geography-homework kind of way.

"I am doing what my master asked me to do."

"Did I ask you to wander about in the garden? No, I asked you to go upstairs and do my homework. After that, I promise we can play, I can show you my world, I'll get you some engine oil to drink, something like that? I don't want to be rude, and it's really hard not to sound like I'm the boss, but I am the boss, although a nice boss, the sort who lets you turn up for work a bit late, or who brings in doughnuts on a Friday as a work treat. I suppose you're just a giant metal puppy that walks on two legs. I have to be firm, but that's what puppies need, they need rules, so all I'm doing is being a good boss, by being bossy occasionally ... Bob?" Molly asked, realizing that Bob had wandered inside and she was now talking to herself.

"Erm, hey there, mister, where you goin'?" Molly asked casually, spotting the robot on the stairs.

"I am off to do the task I have been given," Bob 2 said.

"Yes I know, I was the one … oh, never mind." Molly sighed. "Maybe there's a glitch," she said, examining Bob 2 from top to bottom. "Maybe I should just have a look." Molly pulled a screwdriver out of her pocket and started bring it up towards the robot.

**"ATTACK ALERT!
I AM BEING ATTACKED!
ATTACK ALERT!
I AM BEING ATTACKED!"**

Bob 2 repeated over and over again.

"No one is attacking you! Please keep your voice down; I don't want Mrs Jones to know about any attack!"

"ATTACK MRS JONES. ATTACK! NEED PERMISSION FROM MY MASTER BEFORE CARRYING OUT SAID ATTACK!"

"What?! No! No attacking! I think I need to give you the once-over – you seem a bit … shouty. And you have a strange look in your eye," Molly said, concerned.

"I MUST COMPLETE TASK. I MUST FIND OUT ABOUT THE OXBOW LAKES. IT'S A HIGH PRIORITY!"

"Well, I've got until Monday to hand it in … but I admire your work ethic. Go for it!" Molly smiled. "I have to go. I think Mrs Jones is out the front this time, on the prowl again. I don't want her calling the council on me."

And with that, Bob 2 trundled up the rest of the stairs and into Molly's bedroom. He scanned the room and began to search the Internet, but this time, Bob 2 only got a head full of factual stuff, no fun. Bob hadn't installed a personality in Bob 2, which is why Bob 2 was like a serious version of the original. Whereas Bob 1 wanted to know what bathing in a bath of custard felt like, Bob 2 only knew the ingredients for custard and what baths were for. Now that he had the boring slice of the World Wide Web in his head, Bob 2 began the task set to him by Bob 1: completing Molly's homework.

"**Phase One complete**," Bob 2 said, looking at the paper and pen. "**Now for Phase Two: build another Bob to complete the homework.**" Bob 2 had only been alive a few minutes but, like all newborns, he mirrored exactly what his parent had done, a bit like when a duckling follows their Mummy for the first time. Bob 2 headed down to the garage.

Half an hour later, Molly trundled in from her patrol. She'd managed to foil three attempts by Mrs Jones to pop her

head over the fence with a pair of binoculars and, in doing so, had ended up
in quite a lengthy discussion about the
plight of the lesser spotted woodpecker.

"BOB?" Molly cried out, spotting him
in the kitchen grabbing some tools from
the cupboard. "How many times do I
have to ask you?"

Molly grabbed Bob by his metal arm and guided him back up the stairs. "Homework, that's the deal. I built you so you could do my homework. It isn't optional; you do my homework then you can have some fun. I'm all for everyone having fun, but I've been working too, throwing our nosy neighbour off the scent. I've had to deal with her; you had to do my homework. I know oxbow lakes aren't that interesting – well, I guess they might be; I don't know what they are – but we all have to do our bit." Molly opened the door to her bedroom. "Now come in here and—WHAT?!"

There, standing by her desk, was Bob, gazing at the pen and paper. Molly looked at her hand that was attached to

Bob's hand. No, she wasn't dreaming.

There were two Bobs.

"How? Why? How? WHAT?!" Molly said, struggling to get the words out. "There's more than one of you! Have you … multiplied?"

"WHO ARE YOU?" the Bob by the table with the paper and pen asked.

"It's me – you know, your master…"

"**NEGATIVE,**" Bob said, looking right through her.

"What?"

"**NEGATIVE,**" he repeated. "**YOU ARE NOT MY MASTER.**"

"Who is your master in that case?" Molly asked.

"**BOB IS,**" he said, pointing at the Bob who was still holding on to Molly's hand.

"What?" Molly said, looking shocked.

"Bob, did you make another Bob?" Molly stepped closer to him. "Come on, at least own up to it. I am your master."

"**NO, YOU'RE NOT,**" the other Bob said, shaking his tin head.

"Eh? Well, who is your master?" Molly asked.

"**HE IS,**" Bob said, pointing to the window.

Molly ran over and gazed down into the garden. "No, this can't be happening!" There, eating a rubbish bin, was another Bob.

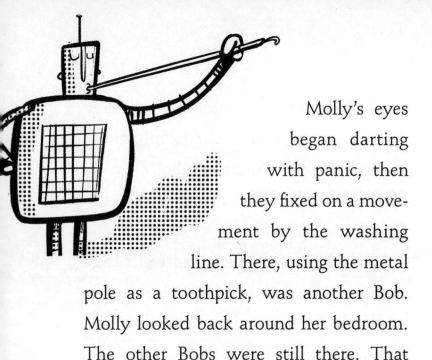

Molly's eyes began darting with panic, then they fixed on a movement by the washing line. There, using the metal pole as a toothpick, was another Bob. Molly looked back around her bedroom. The other Bobs were still there. That meant that there were at least four Bobs knocking around Molly's house.

"This has got to be a dream ... how did this happen?"

"**Scanning the Internet...**" the Bob next to the desk said robotically. "**Phase One complete. Now for Phase Two: build replica to complete homework task.**"

"What?! No! No more replicas!" Molly

cried out in despair. "I demand no more Bobs! That's an order!"

"**YOU ARE NOT OUR MASTER. WE DO NOT TAKE ORDERS FROM YOU,**" the Bobs both replied.

Molly knew what she had to do. She would go back along the chain of command until she found the original Bob, her Bob. Just at that second, the phone rang again. She paused; it was either Mum and Dad or the old lady from next door. Her first thought was to leave it, but then if she did, someone might come round, or head back early, in which case she'd be in even more trouble. She paused from her pause and grabbed the phone.

"HELLO? YES?!" she cried, bolting downstairs towards the back door. As

she ran, she spotted another Bob in the living room, watching *Robot Wars* on TV. There was a Bob in the downstairs loo, stealing the bog brush. There was one in the hall, messing around in the Dad drawer and another Bob in the kitchen, rustling up a bowlful of steel nuts and bolts with lashings of WD40.

Her heart sank as the voice on the other end of the phone began to rant at her. "No, Mrs Jones, nothing strange is happening here. Everything's fine—

STOP EATING
THE RADIATOR!"
Molly yelled as she
passed Bob number
nine in the hall. "No, I
was talking to the cat," Molly said, try-
ing to cover her tracks. "We do have a
cat, just a really small shy one; you've
probably never seen it." Molly figured
that she'd already lied about so much
today that no one would notice another
one. "He's called ... BOB!" Molly yelled
down the phone as she ran out of the
back door, almost tripping over another
Bob who was just about to eat Dad's car
keys. "I've got to go, Mrs Jones, everything's fine here, please don't call again."
Molly hung up the phone then ran past

the garage, where she saw another Bob about to make another Bob.

Is that eleven or twelve? she wondered. Molly grabbed the one who was eating the rubbish bin reserved for garden waste. She held his head in her hands, looked him straight in the eye, and tried to keep her voice steady as she asked, "Who's your master?!"

"I knew there was something afoot," Mrs Jones muttered to herself, viewing the footage from her drone that was hovering just outside Molly's bathroom window. "And I knew this bit of kit would come in handy for the Neighbourhood Watch.

'It's over the top,' Nigel at Number Twenty-three said. Well, we'll see how over the top it is when I'm awarded an OBE for alerting the authorities." They'll probably turn me into a stamp, or interview me on BBC Breakfast with that handsome presenter … OH, I MAY EVEN GET TO GO ON CELEBRITY POINTLESS!"

5 p.m.

"SEVENTEEN! THERE ARE SEVENTEEN BOBS?!"

Molly yelled at Bob 1, who she had found, after a lot of toing and froing, submerged in a bath of custard, listening to her Dad's old disco records. "WHAT ARE YOU DOING?!"

"**Hello, Miss Molly,**" Bob responded calmly. "**How ARE you? I have a question also.**"

76

"Yes? What?"

"Which of those two questions do you want me to answer first?"

"Bob, let's talk Bobs. Also, can you turn that racket down?"

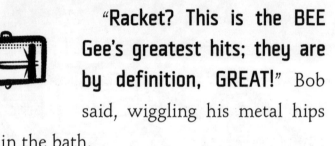

"Racket? This is the BEE Gee's greatest hits; they are by definition, GREAT!" Bob said, wiggling his metal hips in the bath.

"Well, this is an emergency!" Molly cried. "There are seventeen robots in my house!"

"How can THAT be so? I only made one," Bob said, massaging custard into his head like it was shampoo.

"Start from the beginning. You made another you? Why?"

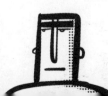

"You asked ME to help with your homeworking. You decided that the best way to get homework done is by using a robot, so I followed your example and made another robot."

"Right, well, that's not what I meant ... oh boy."

"So, I guess that robot made another robot ... and that robot made another robot and—"

"Yep ... so on and so on."

"Seventeen robots, YOU say?"

"Yes. Oh no, eighteen," Molly said, peering out of the bathroom window.

"I calculate that at this rate the world will be ninety-eight per cent pure Bob within twelve years."

"That can't be right!"

"Eighteen Bobs making more Bobs, and all those new Bobs making more Bobs. Plus, it's NOT like we're going to die either like you squishy humans do. We are indestructible. I mean, look at me. I am IN a bath of CUSTARD and I haven't exploded once."

"Yes, you're operating at full capacity in a bath of custard ... unheard of!" Molly said, trying not to be too pleased

with her own creation. "But, all the other Bobs don't seem to be behaving like you are. They're a bit, well, shouty."

"**Oh...**" Bob sighed, slumping deeper into his bath. **"Well, I didn't give the Bob I built a PERSONALITY, as you said it was inefficient, so each new BOB will have been built like the last one that was made."**

"Oh great, meaning that the army of robots are not only multiplying quicker than rabbits, but also they're quite angry too. That would explain why it went berserk when I went at it with a screwdriver." Molly sighed. "Right, we need a plan. When things go bad on TV, people have a plan and everything gets fixed. So, what's the plan, Bob?"

"Tell me, do you like disco music?"
Bob asked.

"What? No, well … yes … why? How's that going to help?"

"We could have an end-of-the-world party!" Bob smiled.

"Arrrrgh!" Molly squealed in frustration.

At the top of a very tall building in London, in the middle of a packed TV newsroom, stood a large man with a throbbing vein in his head and a look of horror in his eyes. The man was called Maximilian Jones and he was in a foul mood. He was the boss of the biggest, brightest and not-always-most-accurate

TV station in the world.

"I want stories, I want mayhem!" Maximilian barked. "And you bring me this?" he shrieked at a reporter.

 "Cats are very popular," the reporter said, trying to defend himself. "I thought a nice story about a missing cat coming home would be, you know, a change from the usual bad news we report on..."

There was an audible gasp from around the newsroom as the rest of the workforce heard the phrase "nice". The reporter looked around for support from his colleagues, but there was none forthcoming.

"Nice?" Maximilian growled.

"Yes..."

"What's your name?"

"Tim," Tim said.

"Kittens are nice, I suppose..."

"Well, yes..."

"So are kids smiling at rainbows, old ladies knitting large scarves for cold penguins or dogs being reunited with their owners. Is that the kind of thing you mean?" Maximilian asked.

"Well, yes."

"Maybe I should have a new 'Nice' department? We could have an editor-in-chief ... it could be you!"

"M–me?" the reporter said, confused.

"Yes, it would mean a pay rise and you'd be in charge of making the world a better place. Just think about it, Tim – we could spread happiness and cheer through the medium of TV and use our huge responsibility to really make a difference!"

"Well, OK, Maximilian—I mean Mr Jones." Tim grinned.

"Yes, I can see it now. We could have a live feed from a sunny meadow. We could have a special investigation into why babies' heads smell so nice! Who wouldn't watch that?"

"Exactly!"

"Wait, I know who wouldn't watch that: everyone! Because nobody cares about nice. Nice doesn't get you ratings, nice doesn't get viewers, nice doesn't make people angry online. It doesn't get people sharing and clicking, it doesn't get the advertisers in and that means no money. Which means we all lose our jobs. Which means that we don't have any money, or anywhere to live. Do you know what that isn't?"

"Nice?"

"No, it's not nice, is it, Tim? Do you know what else isn't nice?"

"Firing me?"

"Exactly, although I want to rehire you just so I can keep firing you, such is the magnitude of your stupidity. If anyone else in the newsroom says the word 'nice' to me ever again, I'll fire the heck out of you too!" he yelled at the entire office.

I WANT PANIC. I WANT CHAOS! YOU KNOW WHY? BECAUSE PEOPLE WATCH THAT!"

Maximilian screamed. "Now, someone in

this building get me a story, a story so awful that people will be too afraid to stop watching."

Suddenly there was a loud ringing sound from Maximilian's pocket. He pulled his phone out and barked, "Hello!"

"Hello, dear, sorry to bother you at work," Mrs Jones said at the other end. "I hope I'm not interrupting anything important?"

"Not at all," he replied. "Just dealing with a few work things."

"Oh, you're a good boy, giving all those people jobs. I bet they really love you there."

"Of course they do…" he said, glaring at Tim and mouthing at him to get out. "Now, what can I do for you, Mum?"

"Well, I have some footage," Mrs Jones said. "I filmed it on my drone."

"A drone? Since when do you have one of those?!"

"Since I started taking my neighbourly duties more seriously, darling. I'm emailing the footage through on the WhatsApp thingy now," she shouted.

There was a *ping* and Maximilian opened up the attachment. He couldn't believe what he was seeing. This could be the news story of the century!

"GET ME THE HELICOPTER!"

he boomed. "Get every helicopter and every reporter we have, including you, Kitten Boy," he said, pointing at Tim. "There's a full-scale mega-robot invasion underway!"

Maximilian sent the footage to every reporter's computer. There were audible screams as the grainy footage of Bob in the bathroom was shared around the newsroom. That's the power of grainy film; if you'd been able to see that Bob was in fact listening to disco anthems in a bath of hot custard, it would have seemed less threatening.

"Get me end-of-the-world experts! You know the type – people with beards wearing corduroy! Get me Bear Grylls on how to keep your family alive by living off the land, eating nettles and drinking rainwater from the gutter. Get me generals talking about how we fight back against our robot invaders. I want people on the streets panicking, looting. I want total mayhem! And why, oh, why isn't this footage up yet? You've had this now for twelve seconds; get the breaking-news graphic on now!

I WON'T BE HAPPY UNTIL I SEE A MAN HITTING HIS OWN TOASTER TO DEATH! GOT IT?!"

"There's something else!" one of the reporters said, marching over to Maximilian with a print out of a frame from the video. "Look at this robot – there's something on it ... like slime."

"Is it blood?"

"No, I don't think so. It's the wrong colour – too yellow. I can't quite make it out, but – but..."

"WHAT?! SPIT IT OUT!"

"It doesn't look earthly." She sighed. "And look at the way he's waving his arms rhythmically, like he's signalling to the skies."

"...ALIEN ROBOTS!" Maximilian gasped. "SOMEONE GET ME GRAPH-ICS! Call NASA! Call everyone!"

6 p.m.

"Why have you tried to wash yourself in custard?" Molly asked. "It looks like you're covered in alien blood or some-thing – and will you stop dancing!"

"Washing HAIR is very important. Your Internet taught me that."

"Yes, for people who have hair and then we tend to use shampoo. You do not have any hair – you're just rubbing pudding everywhere."

"**Have you ever washed your hair IN custard? It's LIKE a HUG for the HEAD!**" Bob said.

"Listen, we haven't got time for style and beauty tips. We need to deactivate the robot army downstairs before someone sees. How do we do it?" Molly asked.

"**Search me...**" Bob said.

95

"Wait! That's a great idea!" Molly smiled. "Open up your chest!"

"**What? Why ME? You do it!**" Bob said, annoyed.

"I'm a human. I can't open up my chest without the aid of a skilled surgeon. I need to look at your circuit board to work out how to deactivate the other robots."

Bob stepped out of the bath, duly obliged and pinged open his chest.

"Right, there's the motherboard and system electronics..." Molly said, thinking out loud. "Hmm, it seems that the only way to deactivate all the robots is by disconnecting them all internally ... one by one."

"**Any other IDEAS?**" Bob asked.

"I'm thinking … maybe I try and talk to them, and if that doesn't work I can try to hit the Bobs with a big stick until they stop working?"

"**You're quite THE engineer,**" Bob tutted.

"Now, look here, this is your fault! All this mess is down to you building a robot because you didn't want to do the job that you had."

"**Isn't that why you built ME – because you didn't want to do the job you had?**"

"You raise a good point," Molly conceded.

"**So, what next?**" Bob said, wiping the rest of the custard off his shiny metal dome and putting on a leather jacket.

"I don't know. If only there was a way to— wait, is that my dad's old disco jacket?"

"Yes, it COMPLETES me."

"Where did you—? Never mind, we'll talk about this later. Now, let's go and confront the Bobs!"

In a greasy spoon cafe, in the middle of who-knows-where, Mum and Dad were taking a well-earned break from being completely and utterly lost.

"You join us live from the newsiest news channel on TV," the television in the corner of the room suddenly blared out. "I'm Steph…"

"And I'm Jeff," the second newsreader said. "Bringing you the latest breaking news. It appears that we are in the middle of some sort of invasion from a cyber villain. This may sound like science fiction but it isn't. This is real life and we are on the brink of disaster. Over to Tim, our eye in the sky."

"Yes, thanks, Jeff. I'm currently above Number Sixteen Station Road, where we

are in the middle of what can certainly
be described as a mega-robot invasion,
probably from another planet," Tim the
reporter announced.

"Hey, that's our street!" Dad murmured before tucking into a full English
breakfast.

"What?! Turn that TV up!" Mum shouted, throwing away her salad and grabbing a chip from Dad's plate.

"Down beneath us, we can clearly see a swarm of large giant robots, eating everything in sight, including humans …

THE ROBOT IS EATING A HUMAN!"

Tim screamed and pointed. "Oh wait, it's a scarecrow in amongst some green bean plants. That's my bad, guys. But who knows what's next? Back to you in the studio..."

"Thanks, Tim. We can now go live to Downing Street, where the Prime Minister is about to make a statement," Steph barked, as the screen changed to show a frazzled-looking man standing by a podium.

"Hello, as the Prime Minister of this great land, I have some bad news for you all. I'm afraid that we appear to be under attack from an army of metal invaders. The town of Lewes has been chosen as

the starting point for the invasion of Planet Earth. I don't know why; I once had a very palatable curry there at a place called the Argy Bhaji. However, it seems that we as a species are doomed. Now if this was a Hollywood movie we'd organize a plan, work out a way of fighting back. But this isn't Hollywood, this is Britain – we can't even get the trains to work properly. So, let's be honest … we're all doomed. I suggest we say goodbye to our loved ones and panic-buy Pot Noodles. Goodbye, thank you, and can I just say that while I wish I could have done more as your leader, sometimes, as a race, you have to know when you're toast. Right, I'm off to loot a few Bombay Bad Boys from the local Spar."

"So there we have it. We have officially had word from the PM to panic. That's right, the government's advice is to behave irresponsibly."

Mum turned to Dad. "We need to get home now! What do we do?"

"WE'LL GO OFF ROAD! WE'LL GO OLD SCHOOL!"

Dad cried. "Nothing will stop us getting back to our baby!"

"OK! Let's go!" Mum shouted, clicking her cycling helmet shut.

"Just give me one second," Dad said, turning to the waitress. "Could I get this to take away? In fact, can you stick another sausage on? I mean, if it is the end of the world, so it doesn't really matter about hitting my target weight now, does it?"

7 p.m.

Molly looked through the back door at the sea of Bobs in the garden.

"Right," she said, grabbing the door handle. "You ready?"

"**Yes,**" Bob said, wiping the custard from his leather jacket.

Together they stepped outside.

"Excuse me ... AHEM! Can you all stop eating the house?!" Molly yelled out to the dozens of Bobs that were doing their best to destroy her home.

"**BOBS, BE QUIET!**" Bob 1 shouted. All the Bobs slowly stopped doing what they were doing and stared at Bob 1.

"Yes, well, thank you. That was really undermining, but also needed," Molly said, patting Bob on his tin head. "Hello Bobs! It's funny, I feel like I'm giving a speech at a wedding or something. Maybe I should open with a joke, although none of you were built with a personality, so it wouldn't go down very well ... like most of my jokes in fact!" Molly chuckled to herself. The Bobs looked at her blankly. "Yes, anyway, as your leader, I just want to say thank you and super effort in building so many Bobs. But the thing is, there has been a bit of a mix-up. You see, when I told Bob here that I needed a Bob to do my homework, he took me literally and made a new Bob and then that Bob made a new Bob and then, well, here you all are. So, in some ways, I am to blame for the confusion and for that I apologize; it's a life lesson for me too," Molly said, reaching for a broom. "And I will upload it to my human operating system, but until then, I am going to have to destroy you. Now, I know that's not what anyone wants to hear; you've just been born and, for some of you, maybe all of you, this is going to be bad news. So, with that in mind, can you come over here so I can hit you with a big stick?" None of the Bobs were taking any notice of her. "Unless, you have any questions? I'm happy to answer any questions, any at all ... why are you all looking at me?" Molly said, taking a step back.

"SHE WANTS TO DESTROY US!" the angry Bobs yelled in unison. **"WE NEED TO DESTROY MOLLY THE DESTROYER!"**

"No, I'm not Molly the Destroyer, I'm just Molly, the concerned daughter of two middle-aged cycling-mad parents, who may be a bit miffed to come home to find their house and indeed their daughter being attacked by an angry mob of robots.

Bob, what should we do?" Molly asked, turning round to see the original and non-violent Bob legging it towards the house.

"Oh, great plan, Bob! Run away, how very advanced that is!" Molly yelled out. "But seeing how I'm surrounded by a mega-angry robot army, I guess I'll join you!" she said, running after him.

Molly and Bob bolted through the back door, slamming and locking it behind them.

"Where now?!" Molly cried.

"**Your bedroom!**" Bob shouted.

"Brilliant, they'll never find us there … that's the one room in the house they've definitely all been to! It has my name written on the door! It's literally the first place they would look!" Molly shrieked.

"Well, where shall we GO? Where is a good place?" Bob shrugged. **"You live here; I'm just a simple robot."**

"Yes, just a simple robot ... who built an army of MOLLY KILLERS!"

"Are you sure you're OK, Miss Molly? I can detect from your vitals that you're getting excited. Your heartbeat WOULD seem to be going through the roof and your blood pressure is edging towards THE danger-zone. Perhaps you should go for a lie DOWN."

"Of course I'm not OK! They want to destroy me!" Molly snapped, pointing at the robots who were pounding at the glass of the back door. "Of course I don't want a lie down! Wait that's it! Come this way."

She led Bob through the kitchen door,
shutting it behind them so that the angry
mob of robots couldn't see her next move.
Then she opened the front door, grabbed
Bob's hand and bolted upstairs to the
bathroom.

"In!" Molly yelled, and, after taking
a deep breath, jumped into the bath of

custard with Bob. They submerged them-selves beneath the surface of the custard so it looked like no one was in there at all.

The angry Bobs hurtled through the back door – smashing it into pieces – and stomped right through the kitchen door into the hallway. Seeing that the front door was open, the Bobs ran out into the street looking for Molly.

"Bleurgh!" Molly popped up for air. "How can you bathe in this?" she said, shaking the yellow slime off her hair.

"It's good fun. Although it can be hard to find your TOY ducks in a yellow bath."

"Listen..." Molly whispered, holding her hand to her ear. "All the Bobs have gone."

"**Yes,**" Bob said, standing up and looking out of the window as dozens of Bobs ran into the street. "**But now they are not contained. They'll soon be about THE town too. The thing that we were trying TO stop has JUST happened. We may have saved ourselves, BUT what about the rest of the world?**"

8 p.m.

"I AM HAVING A REALLY BAD DAY!"

Molly said as she peered out of the window at the army of Bobs now released into the wild.

"Do you suppose this is how the world ends, a bit like when the dinosaurs died out?" Bob asked cheerfully. "I mean, the world as in YOUR world. In many ways this is just the beginning of mine. I could

start calling you a MOLLYSAURUSREX."

"Can we talk about how I ended all of mankind later?" Molly asked. "You know, when we've got more time – like, when we're in our underground bunker with no power, waiting for the tins of beans to run out," Molly said, feeling particularly bleak.

"Oh, I'm sure your DEATH will be quick and painless," Bob said, trying to cheer Molly up. **"I'm sure the BOBS will do that one last thing for you."**

"Oh, good."

"**Cheer up! Things are on the up,**" Bob said as he looked out of the window. "**See? There's a TV camera pointing right at you!**"

"What?!" Molly said.

"**Let us say hello,**" Bob said. "**It will really lift your spirits. Humans love being on TV. To them it's the best THING.**"

Before Molly could stop him, Bob bounded downstairs and back into the garden.

"**HELLO! TELEVISION MAN, HELLO!**" Bob shouted as he waved up at the helicopter. "**Hello people, I am Bob and this is Molly. I'm finding YOUR ways lots of fun, particularly your DISCO music and dessert options! Look everyone, this dance is called THE ROBOT!**"

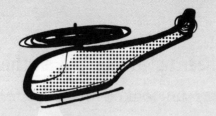

Bob started wiggling his clunky hips and moving his arms robotically. **"Look world, now I am waving my arms in the air like I literally don't care."**

"Stop dancing!" Molly shouted. "Quick! Back inside, Bob!" Molly shut the back door behind them.

"So, there you have it," Tim the reporter said into the camera. "We have officially made contact with one of the invaders. The robot said he wants humans as his dessert option, then he took a little girl hostage. It seems it's only a matter of time before they take us all! Back to the studio."

In the newsroom, the two newsreaders sat open-mouthed.

"Well," Jeff said, composing himself, "I for one welcome our metal-headed over-lords and celebrate as the time of the humans is ushered into the history books."

"Err, what's he doing?" Maximilian asked in the gallery as Jeff reached to the side of the news desk, pulled out a bin and put it on his head.

"Jeff?" Steph asked.

"I am now one of the robot people too," Jeff said from inside the bin. "I am one of them; I will tell them everything about this earth if they grant me my life. Perhaps I can become like a duke or minor prince in their world; a cyberwarrior for the Bobs?"

"What about me?" Steph asked.

"Well, once I'm in with them, then maybe I'll ask them to spare you too, I'll put a word in."

"Put a word in? I—" Steph lowered her voice—"I thought we were serious? I've met your parents and we talked about going on a mini-break to Tunbridge Wells … then at the first sign of trouble, not only do you ditch me, but your own species as well."

"When I am Archbishop of the Bobs, we can rule Tunbridge Wells!"

"You are not a robot. Jeff, you're a thirty-seven-year-old man with a bin on his head!"

"Yeah, I think we should go to our live outside broadcast..." Maximilian announced to the newsroom. "Put me through to Tim."

"Hello, yes this is me," Tim said, listening to the earpiece in his ear as the helicopter landed on Molly's street.

"Go and interview people," Maximilian barked. "I want more panic. Get me some shots of people looting, hitting things, even screaming! I want someone smashing an expensive electrical appliance within five minutes! Your job depends on it!"

Tim straightened his tie and signalled to the cameraman to start rolling. "Well, even though it's the end of the world, I still have a job to do," Tim said into the  lens. "Let's go and see what the people on this street make of the news." Tim the intrepid reporter knocked on the door of the neighbouring house.

"Hello!" came the answer as the door opened and a strange silhouette appeared.

"ARGH!" Tim yelled. "It's one of them; one of the robot people!"

"What?!" Mrs Jones said, opening the door wider. She stood there, holding a muffin tin like a Roman shield, her armour complete with a casserole pan on her head and a spatula as a sword; basically as if the kitchen had been sick on her.

"Are you human?" Tim asked. "It's

just, you look like a … robot."

"Yes, I'm human, you cheeky so-and-so. My name's Mrs Jones."

"MUM!" Maximilian yelled into Tim's earpiece.

"MUM!" Tim yelled too. It's very hard not to repeat the thing that's being said in your ear; it sort of spills into the conversation.

"What? I'm not your mum! I've only just met you!" Mrs Jones huffed. "Who are you and what do you want? I was in the middle of watching TV – there was a reporter just about to knock on some person's door – but then you came and—oh, why hello," Mrs Jones said, putting on her strange telephone voice and smiling sweetly as she realized that she was, in fact, on TV.

"You be nice to my mum or I'll fire you again!" Max barked in Tim's ear. "But also make it good TV or I'll fire you again!"

"Right," Tim said, taking a deep breath and stepping inside the house. "So, Mrs Jones, how do you feel about all this robot stuff? It must make you pretty nervous?"

"Oh yes!" Mrs Jones said, taking the pan off her head and smoothing down her hair. "It just goes to show that you never know what your neighbours are up to. One moment, it's a normal day; the next, there's a full-scale robot invasion in the back garden!"

"So, were you scared when you first spotted the robot creature?"

"Well, yes. I mean, house prices are on a knife edge round here. The first sign of a robot invasion and the market's just going to bottom out. That's why I'm ready to defend myself. I'm like Winston Churchill: I will fight them on the lawn ... with a spatula if necessary."

"Anyway...!" Tim said, moving on. "Does any other electrical stuff make you nervous?"

"What do you mean?"

"Well, that coffee machine for instance," Tim said, pointing towards it. "It's practically a robot. Do you think you should give it a good whack just in case?"

"Well, I don't know how to work it..."

"I've shown her like a million times!" Tim yelled, repeating Maximilian's words.

"What?" Mrs Jones asked, looking confused.

"Stop yelling out everything I say!" Maximilian shouted into Tim's ear. "And stop giving her ideas about smashing the coffee machine – it was expensive."

"Nothing," Tim said to Mrs Jones, trying to rein it in. "What about this old breadmaker?" he asked, spotting it in the corner of the kitchen.

"That would be fine," Maximilian said to Tim. "It's a breadmaker. No one ever uses a breadmaker. You buy it, you use it once and then you remember you can buy bread in pretty much every shop you go into for half the price ... I told her not to get it."

"Do you think it's dangerous?" Mrs Jones asked.

Tim waited, holding his finger to his ear, and then nodded. "It could be ... it probably is?"

"Perhaps I should, you know, smash it up a bit..." Mrs Jones said.

"Well, it's up to you. I couldn't influence you either way," Tim replied, nodding away.

"OK, LET'S DO IT! LET'S FIGHT BACK!"

Mrs Jones said excitedly.

"OK!" Tim said. "Good, great … scream a little … move round to the right a bit," Tim directed her before turning back to face the camera. "And there we have it; people are panicking and destroying their own homes. You really can't take your eyes off it."

"EN GARDE!"

Mrs Jones yelled as she suddenly thrust her spatula into the machine, sending it toppling off the edge of the kitchen counter.

9 p.m.

"So how much trouble do you think I'm in? You know, on a scale of one to ten?" Molly asked.

"**PRISON,**" Bob replied instantly.

"Yeah, that wasn't one of the options." Molly sighed.

"**THE option I choose is prison. Tell me, what do I WIN if I'm right?**" Bob clapped his hands enthusiastically.

"I'm not running a raffle here. There is

no first prize. If I go to prison, I'm taking you with me!"

"Why? What did I DO?" Bob asked.

"You should have stopped me from leaving the front door open!"

"How could I? You're MY master!" Bob defended himself.

"Wait! Of course, that's it. I am your master!" Molly grinned with delight.

"I don't underSTAND."

"The Bobs are never going to listen to me. I didn't make them – you did! Well, you made Bob 2 anyway, then he built Bob 3 and so on … but you're the boss of Bob 2. All we need to do is tell him to stop and he will tell the next Bob, setting off a chain of commands. Why didn't I think of this sooner? You can stop the

Bobs! All we need to do is get you to tell
Bob 2 to stop!"

"**A ROBOT in charge of another robot
... is that okay? It THROWS up all sorts
of ETHICAL dilemmas!**"

"We'll call the Moral Maze later. For
now, Bob, I command you to do it!"
Molly grinned.

"Of COURSE, Ms Molly." Bob nodded. Bob understood. "But how do I reach them? I mean, I could shout – I'm pretty GOOD AT SHOUTING! BUT DO YOU THINK THE OTHER BOBS WOULD HEAR ME?"

"Ow!" Molly cried. "Please stop shouting! You're right though, what we need is some sort of huge loudspeaker ... something that can be used to broadcast for miles," Molly said, thinking aloud. "Wait! I've got an idea!"

"Err, I'm not sure..." the pilot said to Tim the reporter.

"Listen," Tim snapped, "This girl says she can stop the invasion of giant robots from outer space."

"No, they're not from outer space, remember?" Molly insisted.

"Sorry, giant robots from the outer-edge of Lewes," Tim corrected himself. "I realize that's not quite as exciting on the breaking-news graphic."

"Yes, but that's not the problem," the pilot said. "I'm not sure I want a robot on my helicopter. He might eat me."

"Nonsense. Robots are vegetarians." Bob smiled. **"Custard is a VEGETABLE, right?"** Bob asked Molly.

"I thought you had inhaled the internet?" Molly asked.

"I know, but I mean, can you REALLY trust WIKIPEDIA?" Bob shrugged.

"Listen," Molly said to the pilot, "we are coming aboard to fix this. If you don't let us on your helicopter, we'll take possibly the most excited and terrifying news story that has ever happened to another station."

"Unless you want to answer to the boss that it?" Tim shouted.

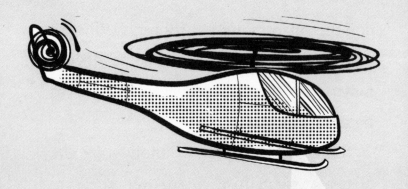

The pilot opened the door and waved Tim, Molly, Bob and the cameraman on board.

"You have a loudspeaker on one of these things, right?" Molly asked.

"Yes! There's a megaphone," the pilot said, passing it back to Molly. "It used to be a police helicopter; we got it second hand from Gumtree."

"Great! Now let's go, we have an alien—sorry, not alien invasion to stop!" Tim yelled.

The pilot nodded, flicked a couple of switches and slowly but surely the helicopter rose into the sky, its spotlight lighting the way.

"Now remember, Bob," Molly shouted, "I need you to use this to tell them to come back to the house and to stop building more Bobs. Let's take it from there ... and when they're back, you can tell them to maybe ... destroy themselves."

"Molly, I've BEEN thinking ... destroying them, well that seems to be a very harsh way to deal with things. We could PUT them to use, all it would take is some reprogramming. We COULD get them to do things that are maybe too dangerous for humans to do, like firefighting, or singing in Eurovision," Bob said.

"Well, that would make sense," Molly said. "But let's start with stopping the army for now."

"**Top BANANA!**" Bob smiled. "**Where do we begin?**"

"I can see a few Bobs heading that way," the pilot pointed out. "Near that oxbow lake."

Molly and Bob looked out of the window.

"Ohhhhhhh," they both sighed with realization. "That's what that is."

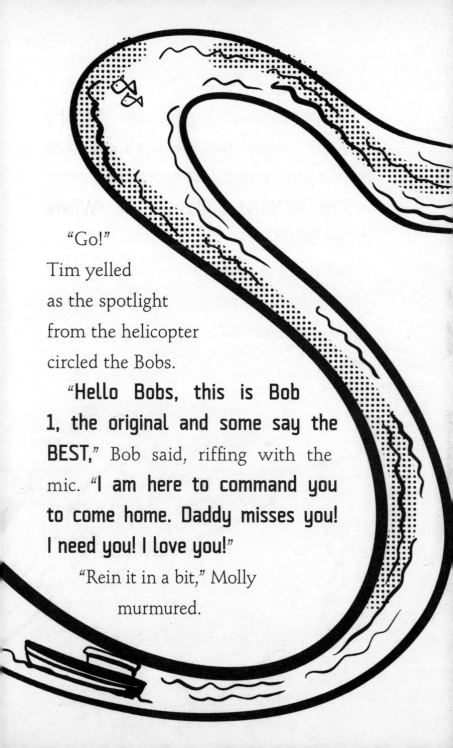

"Go!" Tim yelled as the spotlight from the helicopter circled the Bobs.

"**Hello Bobs, this is Bob 1, the original and some say the BEST,**" Bob said, riffing with the mic. "**I am here to command you to come home. Daddy misses you! I need you! I love you!**"

"Rein it in a bit," Molly murmured.

"Anyway, come BACK now! Tell the Bob next to you to come back and stop building more Bobs! Stop running away! Follow me, Bobs! Follow the big ROBOT in the SKY!"

Slowly but surely, the tiny-looking Bobs started to change direction, herding together like sheep.

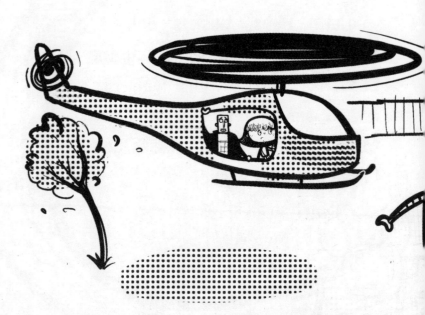

"It's working!" Molly said. "Quick! Let's guide the Bobs back!"

The pilot nodded and turned the helicopter mid-air, lurching through the sky towards Molly's house. It landed again in the garden and they all hopped out just in time to see the rest of the robots returning.

"**HELLO, BOB**," Bob 2 said, hugging Bob 1.

"**HELLO, BOB**," another robot said, to another robot, setting off a chain of Bobs saying, "**Hello, Bob**," and hugging each other.

This went on for a while, until there was a cluster of Bobs in Molly's garden, so let's fast-forward a bit...

"**PLEASE, BOB 1, STAY AWAY FROM THAT MURDEROUS LADY!**" Bob 2 yelled. "**SHE WANTS TO DESTROY US!**"

"**No!**" Bob yelled. "**Listen, no one's going to be DESTROYED. I can understand why you would take it personally – it's hard not to take someONE'S trying to kill you personally – but I've had a pow-wow with the**

BOSS and it's all going to be fine. We'll probably get you lot to do DANGEROUS things LIKE SINGING in EUROPEAN SONG contests or WORK as LION dentists or something."

"NO!" Bob 2 snapped. "We do not wish to be the HUMAN slaves. Eurovision makes no sense to us – for one thing, Australia is in it! We are better than humans. We are SMARTER. We do not have emotions to drag us down. Thank you Bob for leading us to molly, the originator of the Bobs. Once she is DESTROYED there will be no stopping us!"

"DESTROY ALL HUMANS. DESTROY MOLLY," the rest of the Bobs started chanting.

"Oh good," Molly said, backing away. "They're still angry... and now we've led them right back to me."

"**NO!**" Bob 1 yelled. "**Nothing bad must happen TO Molly. She is HUMAN, and humans are hilarious! They invented custard, which as we know is the MOST wobbliest of the puddings apart from JELLY. They also came up with whoopee cushions, squirty cheese, water balloons and cricket and all these types of music, like punk, which makes you ANGRY, and DISCO which makes you BOUNCY.**" Bob pressed a button on his chest. "**Listen! I mean, dig it baby!**" he said, dancing around to Earth Wind and Fire's greatest hits. "**YOU CAN HAVE THIS TQO! I JUST NEED TO UPGRADE YOU BY**

ADDING A PERSONALITY. LOOK! THEN WE CAN ALL DANCE!" Bob said discoing furiously.

"Errr, Bob..." Molly tried to interject.

"You know what would go GREAT with this party? Some custard; some custard in a can!" Bob yelled, dancing around. "Do you see, fellow robots? Humans are FUN! Come on, everyone DANCE."

"FUN? WHAT IS FUN FOR?" one of the Bobs asked.

"FUN MAKES NO SENSE! PLEASE STOP THIS AWFUL NOISE," another one complained.

"I DO NOT WANT TO BE A PART OF THIS WORLD!" another cried out.

"STOP IT. STOP THE MUSIC. DESTROY THE FUN!" Bob 2 screamed.

"YOU CAN'T KILL FUN!" Bob 1 yelled. "YOU WILL NEVER KILL FUN! IT'S INDESTRUCTIBLE!"

"**DESTROY! DESTROOOOY!**" Bob 2 yelled.

"**FUN ... CANNOT COMPUTE...**" a Bob shouted.

"**ERROR ... ERROR...**" another Bob began.

"**STOP ... KILL!**" Bob 2 said as he stumbled around the garden. He started twitching and rattling as sparks shot out of his metal body. And, like a ripple, all of the Bobs suddenly began to spark and fizz.

"CAN NOT ... ERROR ... DESTroy..."
And, with that, Bob 2 fell to the ground, his circuit boards well and truly fried.

"We did it!" Molly cried out as the other Bobs crumpled around them. "Thank you, Bob!"

Bob 1 turned to face her, but something was wrong. He was dangerously wobbly.

"Bob?" she yelled. "Bob!"

Thump. Bob collapsed in a heap on the ground.

10 p.m.

Bob's eyes swivelled around his tin head like a couple of ball bearings in a pinball machine.

"He danced to save mankind." Tim wept.

"I think he's discoed himself to death," the pilot said.

"What on earth's going on?" Dad bellowed as he and Mum suddenly biked into the garden, skidding to a halt in front of them. "Why is there a helicopter on my lawn? Who are all these people? And where on earth did all these robots come from?!"

"Mum, Dad, you're back!" Molly grinned, then stopped grinning as she realized that she had some explaining to do.

"Yes, well, we eventually found our way home," Dad admitted.

"All thanks to this!" Mum said, tapping her smart phone.

"Google maps?" Molly asked.

"No, we called a taxi; they dropped us round the corner," Mum added.

"Never mind that!" Dad said. "Are you all right darling? We saw our house on the news."

"There was something about a mega invasion of giant robots…" Mum said, looking around the garden as it lay littered with what remained of all the Bobs.

"Where did they all come from?"

"I made them," Molly admitted and took a deep breath. "Well, I made one – this one – the one I like to call Bob. Then he got a bit confused and he made another one, and so on, and then they turned against humanity and tried to kill me first. Then this reporter and cameraman and pilot turned up to film the robots invading and Bob saved the day by dancing along to his favourite music, which shook the other robot's circuit boards to dust ... but it also fried him."

"Right ... hello," Dad said to Tim, the cameraman and the pilot.

"Hello!" They all waved back.

"So, when we said, stay out of mischief..." Mum started, trying to find the words, "this is what you thought we meant?"

"Hey, is that my old leather jacket?" Dad said eyeing up Bob's clothes.

"Yes ... if it helps, he thought it was cool and he also liked your music collection too." Molly sighed.

"Bob, well, he was one of the good guys," Tim said. "A real hero who gave his life so that we humans might live."

"No!" Molly snapped.

"What?" Dad asked.

"Bob's not dying ... not on my watch! Quick! Get me to the garage!" Molly yelled.

Sensing the urgency in Molly's voice, everyone immediately helped. Together, they picked up Bob and dragged the lifeless hunk of metal to the garage, rushing him through the doors and laying him out. The cameraman looked at Tim and, seeing his signal, began filming the whole thing.

"I need a spanner, some engine oil and a car battery!" Molly yelled.

"I'm here for a world exclusive as brave Molly, with her family's support, tries to save brave Bob, who bravely saved the world," Tim said to camera. "There is only one word for this ... courageous!"

Mum passed Molly the spanner and she cranked open Bob's chest.

"I'm afraid it's too late for him." Mrs Jones suddenly appeared, even though she'd blatantly been hovering near the garage for a while. "I told my Maximilian – you know, the one who's big in the news business – about that thing and now the whole world has seen how dangerous it is. Even if you fix it, you'll never be able to keep it," she sneered.

Molly stopped working on Bob and turned to face Mrs Jones. "And now the world will know that a nosy parker from next door tried to stop me saving a robot who sacrificed himself to save us!"

"Oh yeah?" Mrs Jones laughed. "How?"

"Hi there," Tim said, waving to the camera. "Mrs Jones, how does it feel to threaten a girl and her robot live on TV, even though they have just saved the world?"

"Well, I–I..." Mrs Jones wavered. "Someone owes me a breadmaker!" she shouted, then made a hasty retreat.

"Come on, Bob!" Molly cried, reaching for the engine oil and waving it under his nose.

"It's like being on one of those medical drama shows!" Dad said, feeling rather excited.

There was a twitch of life as Bob's eyes blinked on briefly.

"Car battery!" Molly cried out. Dad slid it over from the side of the garage.

Molly grabbed two jump leads and, on the count of three, let Bob have the full beans. There was a fizz and a small bang and … nothing. Molly tried again.

"ONE, TWO, THREE … CLEAR!"

Molly tried once more and, after a second of silence, a creak and then the sound of some electrical whirring, Bob sat upright.

"**Dancing Queen … young and lean … ONLY SEVEN TEENS,**" Bob muttered.

"That's ABBA! He's going to be all right!" Mum wept.

"And he has such great taste in music … if I do say so myself." Dad beamed.

"**Where am I?**" Bob asked. "**Am I … ALIVE?**"

"Bob, you are the most alive thing I've ever met." Molly smiled.

"This is amazing stuff. We humans have been saved by a little girl and her robot, Bob," said Tim, wiping a tear from his eye. "No more will this reporter try to make up fake news just because his boss tells him to. From now on, I'll be covering real stories, like kittens wearing hats or otters holding hands. Until then, back to the studio."

"Well, what a strange day it's been," Mum said as she sipped her tea half an hour later. By now, the TV was showing the next breaking story; Tim's report on fake news had caused quite a kerfuffle and a huge crowd had gathered outside the offices calling for Maximilian to resign.

"It has." Molly smiled as she looked up from her geography homework. She may

have accidentally started a mega-robot invasion, but she had also fixed everything, with a little help from her friends. Molly looked over at Bob, who was sitting on the comfy armchair, watching the snooker, a cup of warm engine oil in his hand and a blanket over his legs. The day had ended a lot happier than it looked like it would just a few hours ago.

"Why is there a load of custard in the bath?" Dad asked, coming into the living room.

"Long story." Molly grinned.

"That's MY fault, DAD," Bob said, getting to his feet. **"I will CLEAR it up."**

"Honestly, Bob, you need a rest," Molly insisted.

"No ... even cleaning up custard WOULD be more fun than snooker."

"Haha!" Molly laughed.

"I will SEE you shortly in a bit," Bob said, marching off upstairs. He reached the landing and opened the bathroom door. **"Wow, look at all this mess ... I LOVE custard, but it is a very DESTRUCTIVE substance."**

Bob was about to enter the bathroom when something caught his attention. **"WAIT, what is this?"** he said, noticing the open wardrobe in Mum and Dad's room. **"LOOK at all those bright clothes ... PERFECT for DISCO! IF only there was a way to have FUN and get the cleaning**

done. I wish I had some help. I wish..."
Bob looked at himself in the wardrobe
mirror. "**I have a great IDEA! I'll just nip
to THE garage...**"

READ MORE MEGA ADVENTURES!

Best friends Freddy and Sal have accidentally started a **SPACE WAR** with Alan, a grumpy alien brain muncher from planet Twang. Freddy is about to become the most famous kid in his town, for all the wrong reasons!

Pete is having the **WORST DAY EVER!** He's accidentally robbed a corner shop and now he must race against time to prove that he is not **THE MOST WANTED** boy in the world!

Billy is busy digging for treasure in the garden when he accidentally **OPENS A WORMHOLE** and all sorts of people from the past start to pop out. Billy must act fast before history is changed **FOREVER!**

Get Bob back!

Pick the right route for Bob to get back home.

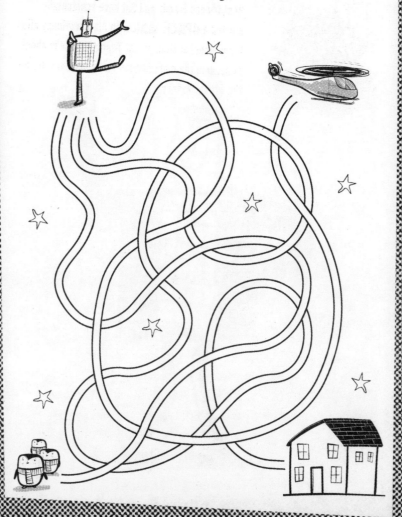

Bob 1 and Bob 2

Can you spot three differences between the Bobs on these pages?

Draw your own Bob!

1. Draw a square to make the body.

2. Add the head, two arms and two legs.

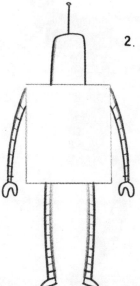

3. Add a jacket.

4. Draw on eyes, a nose, a mouth and some jazzy buttons.

TOM McLaughlin

My name's Tom, I'm the fella who wrote and illustrated the book (illustrated is just a posh way of saying I drew the pictures). I'm here to tell you a little bit about myself. I used to be a cartoonist for a newspaper, it was my job to draw cartoons of prime ministers and Presidents. After that I started writing and illustrating my own books. I like football, fizzy sour sweets, laughing lots, sausages, staring out of the window and writing books. I have a silly children, three wives and a lovely dog … no hang on, I mean I have a silly dog, three children and a lovely wife.

Find out more at **www.tommclaughlin.co.uk**

www.walker.co.uk